Butterflies

Butterflies

a novel

Mary Longley

atmosphere press

© 2022 Mary Longley

Published by Atmosphere Press

Cover design by Kevin Stone

No part of this book may be reproduced without permission from the author except in brief quotations and in reviews. This is a work of fiction, and any resemblance to real places, persons, or events is entirely coincidental.

atmospherepress.com

Harlem, New York

1964–1965

*The coming-of-age story of three 17-year-old best friends
Violet Johnson, Cecily Brooks, and Shirley Williams.*

Ode to Harlem

*They migrated north, looking to leave behind those dusty trails and
the banality of that tired ol' separate and unequal and found
themselves in a vibrant town called Harlem.*

*The cotton there was a club where the precious voices of Ella and
Louis blew the roof off the segregationist policy with talent
too rich to deny.*

*There would be a renaissance where Langston reminded the status
quo that, I Too, Am America and Zora's Eyes Were Watching God
whose eyes were watching all.*

*Here the uncaged like Maya penned Africa and the fiery voice
of Malcolm extolled African.*

Preachers ruled the roost with an iron fist of morality.

*Parents worked hard to make ends meet and when things got
Bumpy those in that life controlled the streets.*

*Harlem's Mr. Smith was Mr. Powell, who went to Washington,
activating his activism in the capitol city built by his forefathers.*

In Harlem, three young women came of age,

Learning from family

Embracing friendship,

Discovering love.

Here in Harlem, they became

Butterflies.

Chapter 1

September 1964

"*Violet!* Girl, come eat your breakfast before it gets cold!" shouted her mother, Ida Mae Johnson. "Every Saturday, it's the same thing with her coming to breakfast late cause she's reading those plays or writing a new poem," said her exasperated mother.

"Your sister Sarah's the one got Violet all caught up in those plays and writing poetry. She says Violet has a creative mind," said Violet's father, Robert Johnson Sr.

Ida Mae set out three plates of savory sausage, fluffy scrambled eggs, and buttery toast, along with coffee and orange juice. She and Robert Sr. were in the kitchen of their modest Harlem apartment, waiting for Violet to join them at breakfast. They were seated on green, yellow, and white floral cushioned wooden chairs around a matching oval table covered with a white linen tablecloth. To the side of the table was a wide, high window decorated with yellow and white embroidered swag curtains. Behind the table in the compact kitchen stood a white stove, and above it, a porcelain white plaque with the famous house prayer by writer Helen Taylor—*Bless This House Oh Lord We Pray, Keep it Safe By Night and Day.*

"She ought to be figuring out what college she's attending, not focusing on foolishness," said Ida Mae. "Everybody can't be Maya Angelou."

"She's still a girl, Ida Mae, let her have some fun," said Robert Sr. "School just started, and she already said she was applying to Spelman College, to be near Robbie at Morehouse," he said proudly.

Ida Mae gave her husband an incredulous look and said, "I don't recall you being so gentle with Robbie when he was a senior."

"Robbie's a boy, and one day he'll have a family to support. Violet will marry a man who will take good care of her," Robert Sr. said with conviction.

Ida Mae gave her husband a sharp look but bit her tongue. She was preparing her daughter to take care of herself, husband or no husband.

Seventeen-year-old Violet Johnson was in her bedroom, which she decorated in hues of violet in homage to her name. She was lounging on a chestnut framed bed covered with a frilly violet bedspread that was speckled with white flowers. Above the bed was a framed picture of violet flowers flowing out of a clear vase that she sketched and painted herself. On the wall opposite her bed sat a chestnut dresser. On the right side of the dresser was a framed picture of a smiling infant Violet sitting in a pink highchair. On the left side were several Jet magazines fanned out in a semi-circle, and in the center of the dresser was a jewelry box containing bangle bracelets, earrings, and other personal knickknacks. To the right of her bed was a matching chestnut bookcase filled with mystery books, poetry, and plays by famous African American writers.

Violet had smooth brown skin the color of freshly picked pecans, and brown eyes the shape of almonds. She wore a blue flared-legged dungaree jumper over a short-sleeved black t-shirt, and her shoulder-length black hair was styled in a ponytail. Lying on her bed swinging her right foot to and fro, she was engrossed in a book by famed author James Baldwin titled *Go Tell It On The Mountain.*

The book secretly gifted to her by her Aunt Sarah was loosely based on the author's life and touched on race, religion, and morality. Violet and her aunt considered themselves kindred spirits who shared a love of poetry and plays and were also passionate about women's rights and civil rights.

At the sound of her mother's exasperated shout, she put away the forbidden book, donned her favorite Chuck Taylor sneakers, and ran to the kitchen. It was Saturday, and she wanted to hang out with her best friends Shirley and Cecily. "No sense in making mama mad," she thought.

Chapter 2

Shortly after breakfast, Violet went to meet up with Cecily and Shirley, who had been sitting on the stoop of her apartment building waiting for her to come downstairs. The girls all lived within five blocks of each other. Shirley and Cecily were dressed identically to Violet in blue denim jumpers, black t-shirts, and black converse sneakers.

Cecily had light honey brown skin, wide medium-blue eyes, and she wore her hair in long stylish black braids.

Shirley who was a few shades darker than Violet had golden-brown eyes framed by long dark eyelashes and her hair was styled in a thick afro puff. The friends represented a rainbow of blackness.

Violet and Shirley were born and raised in Harlem, while Cecily migrated with her family to the region five years earlier from South Carolina.

"We should go searching for butterflies," said Cecily.

"Girl, ain't no butterflies around here in Harlem," said Violet, giving Cecily a critical look.

"Told you she touched," said Shirley.

"I am not touched," said an indignant Cecily. "I saw butterflies in that empty lot."

The abandoned lot, two blocks from Violet's apartment building, took center stage in the life of the local residents. It held an array of discarded items, including an old bicycle frame, whisky bottles and a rusted out 1950s Caddy. Despite its abused state, there was a natural beauty to the lot where overgrown weeds and flowers sprouted out the dank earth.

"We're too old to be chasing after silly ol' butterflies," said Shirley with annoyance. "Let's go roller-skating." She knew Violet found Cecily's optimism endearing, but she saw Cecily as someone afraid to face reality. After Shirley's father died and her mother became a single parent, she had to grow up fast. Pretending that life was all rainbows and sunshine wasn't a luxury she could afford.

"Cecily, the only thing in that lot is an abandoned car and overgrown weeds," said Violet. "You are not in the south anymore. This is Harlem, and no one around here searches for butterflies. I agree with Shirley, we should go roller-skating."

Cecily approached Shirley, who was beginning to get on her nerves with her negativity and said, "Adults study butterflies for a living, Shirley, so no, we are not too old to search for them." Turning to Violet, she said, "You can find butterflies anywhere if you open your eyes and look. Here, I bought a net and jar that I poked holes in so the butterfly will have air to breathe," she said, showing them her butterfly-catching items.

Violet stared at Cecily as though she had completely lost her mind.

Shirley half-whispered to Violet, "Touched, I tell you."

Frustrated at what she saw as their lack of adventure and open-mindedness, wagging her finger, Cecily snapped, "Now look here, Shirley, I am not touched!" Giving Violet a fierce squinty look she said, "I went with you and your aunt to that Minister X rally last year. My mama and daddy would have had a fit if they'd known I was there. Mama likes him, even though most say he's a rabble-rouser, but daddy prefers Minister King."

"I swear Cecily, you can't keep a secret!" shouted Violet, angered at having her extracurricular activities revealed.

"Shirley, let's go so we can show her there ain't no butterflies in Harlem," said Violet, heatedly stomping down the street, eager to prove Cecily wrong.

Protesting, Shirley said, "We should go roller-skating or to my house and listen to the Temps and Supremes, not chasing after something that doesn't exist. We're too old for this silliness."

Whispering to Violet, Shirley asked, "You went to that speech? You some radical now?"

"Just come on, Shirley," said an exacerbated Violet, refusing to answer questions about her political views.

The girls walked around the abandoned lot in search of Cecily's elusive butterfly.

"I don't see any butterflies, but I see big, nasty flies buzzing around," said a horrified Shirley.

"They're out here, keep looking," said Cecily.

"I'm with Shirley," said Violet. "We are not going to find any butterflies out here."

"Keep looking, Violet," said Cecily, searching high and low and getting annoyed that her friends didn't believe her. Then her eyes landed on something fluttering in the weeds. "Look, right there!" she said excitedly, scooping up the butterfly with her net.

Violet could not believe her eyes. Right there in Harlem, in an abandoned lot near a rusted-out car, surrounded by weeds, was a black and gold butterfly fluttering around in the sunshine. She stared at Cecily who was gently placing the butterfly in a glass jar.

Cecily, the cheery optimist, was right. You could find beauty anywhere if you were willing to look for it.

Chapter 3

"This is a female Black Swallowtail butterfly," said Cecily. "Females have smaller spots than males and more blue scales on their wings," she said, examining her find.

The girls were in Cecily's bedroom, which was decorated the color of sunshine, and matched her sunny, optimistic personality and love of nature.

"It's a shame that I have to let her go," said Cecily.

"Let who go?" asked a distracted Violet, lying on Cecily's carpeted floor, reading a flyer about the upcoming tryouts for the school play *A Raisin in the Sun*.

"The butterfly," said Cecily.

Violet turned her head towards Cecily and said, "So what was the point of capturing the thing if you're going to free it?"

Shirley, who had been flipping through a fashion magazine, looked up, winked at Violet, and pointing to her head, whispered, "Told you so, touched."

"She belongs in nature, not trapped in a jar," said Cecily, cooing lovingly at the butterfly.

Violet shook her head. Cecily rarely made sense, but she liked her friend's hopeful outlook on life.

"Well, you two can go back to the lot if you want, but I have to get home and finish my school project," said Shirley.

"What's your project on?" asked Violet.

"Negro women in the suffrage movement," said Shirley.

"Not only were they fighting against male domination, but they also had to battle against white women of the suffrage movement who didn't see Negro women's struggles as equal to theirs. They still don't," she said with a shrug.

Violet was surprised. She had no idea Shirley was interested in social causes, which is why she didn't tell her about the rallies she attended with her aunt. Shirley had always avoided anything too controversial that might interfere with her future. Violet was happy to know that they were of the same mindset.

"Shirley Williams, women's rights activist!" said Violet.

"Got that right," Shirley said, raising her fist in the air as she sauntered out of the room.

Chapter 4

Sitting cross-legged on Cecily's bedroom floor, Violet said, "I'm going to try out for the role of Beneatha in *A Raisin in the Sun*. I heard that Johnny is trying out for Asagai."

It was common knowledge that Violet had a crush on Johnny Richardson.

Cecily rolled her eyes. For the life of her, she didn't understand Violet's interest in Johnny. He was a jock with nothing to say outside of "hut, hut" during football season and "pass me the ball man" during basketball season. Now, his friend...

Staring at herself in the mirror as she practiced her pirouette, Cecily said, "I already signed up for that role. You can try out for Ruth or Mama instead."

Uncrossing her legs and getting up from the floor, Violet reached for her green canvas purse and pulled out her well-read copy of the play, tossing it on the dresser next to Cecily.

"My aunt Sarah gave me a copy of the play and I like the character of Beneatha. She's determined, like me, and that's the role I'm trying out for. *You* can try out for Mama or Ruth."

Unperturbed, Cecily said, "I'm a dancer, a natural performer, and I'd be great in the role. Performing is in my blood."

"I'm an artist, and I've been reading and acting out plays with my aunt all my life," said Violet, "so I guess that means it's in my blood too."

"You draw art, I perform it, which means I have the talent for this role," Cecily said huffily, tossing her long braids dramatically.

"I have the best reading voice in our English class, even Ms. Polly said so," retorted Violet.

"You're pretty good," Cecily said dismissively, "but I'm light on my feet and plan to be an Alvin Ailey Dancer in the near future."

"You haven't even tried out for Alvin Ailey, and besides, this play is mostly dialogue, with very little dancing," snapped Violet.

All thoughts of perfecting her pirouette forgotten, Cecily, both hands on her hips, walked over to Violet and said, "If you were really my friend, you wouldn't try out for a role that you know I want."

"I have just as much right as you to try out for Beneatha, Cecily."

"You're wasting your time Violet, I'm a shoe in for that role."

"I guess we'll see. Let the best actress win," said Violet, grabbing her play and stuffing it back into her purse before rushing out of Cecily's bedroom, and slamming the door shut in her wake.

Cecily raced behind Violet, opened the door, and shouted, "That will be me!" before slamming it shut again.

Chapter 5

Violet spent the rest of the weekend rehearsing for the role of Beneatha.

"How did I sound, mama?"

"You sounded good, baby, like a real, honest-to-goodness actress," said Ida Mae.

Truthfully, Ida Mae was half-listening. She was darning her husband's work pants, wondering how he managed to get so many holes. "Time for some new pants, husband, cause I'm tired of patching these up." She knew he would rather wear patches than miss a tuition payment for Robbie. Ida Mae loved her family and the life they had, but she'd be lying if she didn't admit that she wished that the so-called *American Dream* would trickle down their way.

Ida Mae and Robert Sr. worked hard to provide for their family but only seemed to break even, just getting by. She wanted a house like her cousin Thelma and her husband Nathaniel. They were living the good life on Long Island, but she reckoned it was easy to live good when you didn't have children to provide for.

Thelma and Nathaniel wanted children but weren't able to have any. "I s'pose the saying is true. You can't always have it all," she thought. Thelma and Nathaniel were very generous to the children in their extended family during birthdays and holidays, including Violet and Robbie. Ida Mae said a silent prayer of contrition for her envy and asked God to bless Thelma and Nathaniel with children of their own.

"All finished," she said, snipping the thread.

"Was I convincing, showing my anger at Walter?" asked Violet.

"Hmm? Oh yeah, baby, you told that Walter off good. Had me believing it was real," said Ida Mae.

"Mama, you weren't listening. I was talking to Asagai about Walter. I wasn't talking to Walter," said a frustrated Violet.

"And you did a fine job too," said Ida Mae, putting the needle and thread back into the old cookie tin where she kept them along with her crochet needles.

Violet gave her mother a dubious look but softened when she saw the weary look on her face.

"Mama's probably worrying about money again," she thought. She knew that even though her parents worked hard money was always tight. Violet wanted to get a part-time job, but her parents said she needed to focus on school now because work would dominate her entire adult life.

Looking at her mother lovingly, she thought, "It won't always be this hard, mama, I promise you." Knowing there wasn't anything she could do to immediately alleviate her mother's burden, she went back to rehearsing for the school play.

Chapter 6

"You two are acting so silly," Shirley said to Violet as they walked down the hallway of their public high school, passing by a colorful bulletin board littered with upcoming school activities.

The hallway at Harlem High was full of chatter as students rushed to their third-period classes.

"You and I have been friends since the sandbox, so you have to side with me," said Violet.

Shirley took in Violet's black pants, black blouse, and black beret tilted militantly on her head but said nothing of her friend's slightly radical look. Shirley was fashionably dressed in black pants with a frilly white top and flat black shoes.

Responding to Violet, she said, "That's not fair. We've been friends with Cecily since she moved here five years ago. You and Cecily act like you're trying out for a role on Broadway. The two of you can't let a high school play destroy your friendship."

"Don't you mean our friendship?" retorted Violet.

"*Don't you dare put me in the middle of this mess,*" snapped Shirley. "I'm going to be friends with both of you regardless of who gets that stupid role."

"I have to get to history class. *Make-up with Cecily,*" Shirley said sternly, brushing past Violet.

Later that afternoon, students assembled in the auditorium to try out for *A Raisin in the Sun*. Excited chatter filled the air as the students waited to read for their desired role in the play.

"Hello everyone, can I please have your attention?" asked Ms. Polly, raising her voice to be heard over the boisterous teens. "Please settle down and take your seats. We are here for the final tryout for our play."

"Not surprising, Beneatha was the most sought-after role," said Ms. Polly. "The read-through will begin with a scene between Beneatha and Asagai."

Ms. Polly, the high school English and drama teacher, was a tall, pretty woman with smooth dark chocolate skin. She had a wide mouth and full lips that always displayed a friendly smile. Ms. Polly was clothed in black and gold Afrocentric pants, with a matching top and a black head wrap. Her ears were adorned with long gold leaf goddess earrings, and she had a large gold cuff bracelet on her right wrist.

Ms. Polly began by explaining the scene between Beneatha and Asagai. She spoke with passion, waving her hands around for dramatic effect.

"Born in the voiceless age of womanhood, twenty-year-old college student Beneatha is blazing mad. Her dream of becoming a doctor has evaporated in a puff of smoke," she said, snapping her fingers, "after her older brother Walter squandered away the family's inheritance."

"Please note her name, everyone. Beneatha is an African name, meaning beauty, and beneath her."

"First up is Cecily Brooks, who will be reading with Johnny Richardson, who won the role of the Nigerian born college student, Asagai."

The students hooted and hollered their congratulations at the lanky teen. Johnny feigned embarrassment before taking a melodramatic bow.

Getting into character, Cecily, dressed in a vibrantly colored orange and purple African dress, sashayed across the stage. Johnny stared on, entranced by her movements. Violet, sitting in the audience, taking it all in, rolled her eyes at what she saw as Cecily's overly dramatic behavior.

Ms. Polly raised her hands high above her head before bringing them down in a sweeping motion and said, "Begin!"

Cecily/Beneatha: He made an investment! With a man even Travis wouldn't have trusted with his most worn-out marbles.

Johnny/Asagai: Gave it away?

Cecily/Beneatha: Gone!

Johnny/Asagai: I'm very sorry...And you, now?

Cecily/Beneatha: Me? ...Me? ...Me, I'm nothing ...Me. Asagai, while I was sleeping in that bed in there, people went out and took the future right out of my hands! And nobody asked me, nobody consulted me—they just went out and changed my life!

Johnny/Asagai: Was it your money he gave away?

Cecily/Beneatha: It belonged to all of us.

"And, cut! Well done, Cecily. Next up is Violet Johnson," said Ms. Polly.

As Violet approached the stage, she exchanged glances with Cecily. Though the hostility between the two had waned, neither girl was willing to make the first move towards reconciling, which was why Shirley chose not to attend the audition, preferring to stay out of the conflict.

Violet took her place on stage and for the first time, reassessed her all-black ensemble. Each time she read the play, she saw Beneatha as strong and rebellious and assumed dressing in all black would fit the character's personality. However, after seeing Cecily frocked in the African dress, she realized she might have misinterpreted Beneatha, instead visualizing her own political views onto the character. Clearly, the play showed that Beneatha's relationship with Asagai brought her to embrace African culture. Thinking back to her argument with Cecily, Violet had to admit that she hadn't familiarized herself with the characters as much as she had with the dialogue.

Putting that aside, for now, she got into character, smiling nervously at Johnny, who offered a friendly smile in return, though nothing close to the drooling look he had given Cecily.

Digging deep inside herself to bring alive Beneatha's heartache and frustration, she drew on the anger she felt yesterday during her argument with Cecily, the weary look of her mother fretting over the family's finances, and the indignities faced every day by Negro people simply trying to get ahead.

Violet passionately hammered out her lines and was surprised when Ms. Polly yelled, "Cut!" She had immersed herself so deeply into the character that she'd lost all sense of self and Johnny too. It felt as though a curtain had opened, and light poured in as her focus returned. She looked up to see Johnny staring awestruck at her as the auditorium erupted in applause at her performance.

Violet smiled and did a mock curtsy. She perused the crowd, her eyes landing on Cecily, whose shocked expression told her all she needed to know. "I nailed it!" she thought, walking off stage. "Hmm, maybe I should consider acting rather than law."

Since she was a little girl, she had wanted to be a lawyer, impressed with Thurgood Marshall's fight for civil rights and Charlotte Ray's audacity at becoming the first Negro female lawyer during a time when women, especially Negro women, weren't welcomed in law schools. However, for the first time in her life, Violet was unsure what career path to pursue.

Soon after the last girl auditioned, Ms. Polly announced that she decided who would play the coveted Beneatha.

"Settle down everyone, our cast is complete," she said cheerfully. "Thank you to everyone who tried out for the play. Lorraine Hansberry would be so proud of your enthusiasm. Now, without further ado, the character of Beneatha will be played by Regina Bolds."

Everyone congratulated Regina, who was smiling from ear to ear.

"I hope to see all of you here on opening night supporting your classmates," said Ms. Polly. "I'd like my *Raisin* cast to stay on so that we can go through the rehearsal schedule," she said, fluttering around like Diana Sands, the actress who originated the role of Beneatha on Broadway.

Violet and Cecily locked eyes and smiled sheepishly. Their iceberg melted.

Chapter 7

October 1964

"He is so fine," said Violet, dressed in blue dungarees, a blue and white top, and her favorite black Chuck Taylor sneakers. She was staring across the cafeteria at Johnny, who was animatedly talking and roughhousing with his friends.

Cecily and Shirley turned in their seats to look at him.

Shirley, dressed in blue jeans, a white top, and black converse sneakers, rolled her eyes. Like Cecily, she didn't understand Violet's attraction to Johnny, whom she found shallow.

Cecily, wearing blue jeans, paired with a black and white top and the same footwear as her friends, said, "He's not that cute," before biting into her cheeseburger.

The girls were on break, eating lunch in the crowded and noisy cafeteria.

"Hurry up, so we can go outside," said Shirley, "Nobody wants to sit here all lunch period watching you moon over Johnny Richardson."

"Ain't nobody mooning over Johnny," Violet said defensively. "Besides, he's cuter than that ol' Trent, you love so much."

"There's Trent now. *Hey Trent,*" said Shirley, waving furiously.

Trent blushed and nodded his head in acknowledgment,

before walking over to where his friends Johnny and Martin were seated.

"Fine, strong and muscular," said Shirley, drooling over Trent.

Violet, who knew that Shirley liked Trent, was none the less surprised at her bold display. Giving her friend a critical look, she asked, "Now, who's mooning?"

Getting up from the table to throw out her trash, Cecily said, "Martin's smarter than both of them and gets better grades."

Violet and Shirley stared after Cecily, who rarely showed interest in any of the boys at school.

Heading towards the exit before any comment could be raised about her interest in Martin, Cecily asked, "Y'all coming or what?"

The girls were outside in the schoolyard, standing by one of the lone trees. Unlike the public schools in the more affluent neighborhoods downtown, the public schools in Harlem had few recreational resources to entertain the students during their break. There was, of course, the obligatory basketball court with a rim containing no netting for swishing.

"Let's go to the movies this weekend," said Violet.

"There's nothing good out right now. We could go roller-skating," said Shirley.

"I'll have to see how much money I have left over after I pay for the latest senior fees," said Cecily.

"Girl, say it again," said Shirley. "My mama said if I ask for one more dollar to pay those fees, she's going to send me to live at that school, since that's where all our money is going."

Violet and Cecily laughed, having pretty much heard the same thing from their parents.

"At least y'all got two parents. My mama has to do it all alone," said Shirley.

Knowing that Shirley had it even harder than her and Violet, Cecily said, "Money's tight at our house too, but Travis sent me a little extra cash that I was saving to buy new ballet slippers for my dance audition. I should have enough left over to pay for us to go skating."

"How's he doing over there in Nam?" asked Violet.

"I'm not really sure," said Cecily. "When Travis writes, he doesn't say a lot about his experience. Daddy and mama are concerned. Daddy said he remembers his time in the Great War, and it was none too pretty. The men he served with refused to share the gory details with their family. Daddy said they glorify it to sell you on the service, but it's eye-opening when you're in the thick of it."

The bell rang, ushering the girls back to class.

Violet was happy because the look on Cecily's face said she was worried about Travis, too.

Chapter 8

"I mailed off the last of my college applications," said Violet. "Spelman's my first choice, and I added Howard as a backup. Since Robbie's attending Morehouse, I'll have someone nearby in Georgia," she said. "I don't think mama and daddy would have agreed to me going to school in the south if Robbie wasn't already down there."

Rather than going roller-skating as originally planned, the girls went to Shirley's apartment to hang out. They played music, ate pizza, and downed milkshakes. Shirley's apartment had an earthy vibe, with various African art pieces, prints, and cloths decorating the rooms, all of which reflected her mother's personality and style.

"Good choice," said Shirley. "What do you plan on studying?"

"Whatever courses they offer so I can become a civil rights lawyer," said Violet.

Cecily said, "Look out, Violet's headed to the Supreme Court. All those Malcolm X rallies have gotten to her."

Violet smiled and said, "I hope to be a lawyer, but you know they ain't letting no Negro woman on the Supreme Court." *Cough* "I was thinking about taking a few drama classes. You know, keep my options open."

"Got the acting bug after that play?" asked Shirley.

"It made me think about other options for sure," said

Violet. "I have to be realistic, not box myself in. Life as a Negro female attorney won't be easy. Why not study both? Maybe even do some acting on the side. Who knows, we'll see," she said.

Shirley nodded her understanding and said, "Spelman is my first choice too, but I also applied to Howard. I added Fisk because mama likes their history. W.E.B. Du Bois attended the school, and that freedom rider, John Lewis, who's doing those sit-ins goes there. I'm not sure we can afford any of them," she said sadly.

Violet asked, "Can't you take out a loan?"

"Mama's looking into it, but you know it's not easy for Negros to get those loans, and it'll probably be even harder since it's just her applying," said Shirley, wishing her father was still alive.

"So, apply to a local college," said Cecily. "Spelman and Fisk are in the south. You don't want to be anywhere near the south. I'm never going back," she said with conviction.

Violet and Shirley knew that Cecily and her parents experienced a lot of hardship and racism in the south, which is why they moved north. The friends knew it was also a sore spot of Cecily's and avoided the subject as much as possible. Unfortunately, with so much news coming out of the south about segregation, the marches, church bombings like what happened with those four little girls in Birmingham, Alabama shortly after Cecily moved north, it was hard to avoid.

Shirley didn't want to upset her friend, but she needed to know what life would be like for her and Violet in the south.

Gingerly, Shirley said, "I know you don't like talking about your time in the south, but if me and Violet get into one of those schools, we'd at least like to know what to expect. Can you tell us a little about life down there, Cecily?"

Cecily sighed and said, "If it will make you reconsider staying in the north, I'll share some things with you, but afterward, I don't want to discuss it again."

"We promise we won't bring it up again," said Shirley.

Violet was happy that Shirley asked because she was dying to have a current account of life in the south. Her parents left Georgia shortly after getting married and moved in with her mother's cousin Thelma and her husband Nathaniel who were living in Harlem at the time. The majority of Negros who moved north followed already established family members.

Cecily said, "Everything you heard about the south and segregation is true. Kind of like it is right here in Harlem, but without all the 'Whites Only' signs."

Shirley and Violet glanced at each other, taken aback by Cecily's statement. They never saw their living situation as segregated, but in hindsight, Cecily was right. Since they lived in a predominantly Black neighborhood, they were sort of cocooned from the realities of segregation. In truth, it was the north's version of segregation.

Violet wondered how she failed to recognize how pervasive it was in her own life when she attended the rallies and her parents often spoke of the slights they faced at work.

"Malcolm X speaks about it all the time," said Violet.

Cecily nodded her agreement and continued. "It's best to be indoors before it gets dark to avoid trouble...No matter how old you are, they will always address you as girl and boy. You can't look them in the eye, because somehow making eye contact is seen as disrespect. Even the kinder white folks make sure you stick to the rules and will never let you forget that you're a Negro first and above all."

Violet and Shirley grew quiet hearing Cecily confirm what they had assumed.

Attempting to lighten the mood, Violet said, "You never said what schools you applied to, Cecily."

"I don't think I'm going to college," said Cecily. "I want to become a dancer and tour the world like Maya Angelou did. I don't want to be stuck in one spot, and I sure don't want to be cleaning up after people or working in some office," she said.

"Even though Travis doesn't talk about his life in the military, he said he likes traveling and meeting people with different attitudes than those here in the states."

"You can study dance at college," Shirley said sternly. "At least you have the chance to go with two working parents."

"My parents don't make that much money, which is why Travis went into the military," said Cecily. "Besides, even with my mama and daddy working, that don't mean those folks giving us loans. Negros just got civil rights and like daddy said, had to fight like hell for that, and still not much has changed."

"Eventually, it has to. It's the law," said Shirley.

"When has the law mattered when it came to rights for us?" asked Cecily.

Violet said, "You should think carefully, Cecily. You don't want to look back and wish you had gone to college. Not to be a jinx, but you could get injured. At least with college, you'll have options. That's why I'm also taking drama classes."

"Violet is right," said Shirley. "If I were you I wouldn't put all of my eggs in one basket."

"Well, I'm not you, and I know what I want. I want to dance," Cecily said with finality, ending all discussion on her career choice.

Chapter 9

November 1964

"I'm so excited, Robbie's coming home today," said Violet.

"Yes, and I'm sure he'll bring piles of laundry," said a beaming Ida Mae.

"And you can't wait to do it for him," said Robert Sr., also smiling broadly. "I'm looking forward to seeing our boy, too. One more year, and he'll be the first in our family to get a college diploma," he said with pride.

"He'll be in his last year at Morehouse as I'm heading to Spelman," Violet said gleefully.

"Two kids in college," thought Robert Sr. with both a happy and concerned sigh. He didn't know how he and Ida Mae would swing two college payments, but they'd figure it out he supposed.

Robert Sr. began to reminiscence over his conversation with Ida Mae about affording the kids' college.

"All I did was suggest that Violet wait a year, just until Robbie graduated, since money was tight and all, and Ida Mae refused to speak to me for a week and even slept on the couch!" he recalled with horror. "Thank goodness Violet didn't notice none since Ida Mae always rose first in the morning."

When Ida Mae started speaking to him again, she said, "Now look a here husband, you are not to treat Violet no different than Robbie. As a Negro woman, she needs to be able to fend for herself, not just depend on a husband to save her, not that there's anything wrong with that."

Robert Sr. admitted he was old-fashioned and thought it was a man's place to take care of his family. "Truth be told, if Ida Mae hadn't worked all them years as a nurse's aide, I'm not sure our family would have survived on my porter's salary alone, so maybe she does have a point. Either way, I don't like my wife not speaking to me and sleeping on some couch. It ain't right. Violet is going to college and that's that. We'll make a way somehow."

Later that evening, Violet and her parents drove to the train station to pick up Robbie. The station was bustling with travelers arriving and leaving to celebrate Thanksgiving with family and friends. After discovering what track Robbie was due to arrive on, they positioned themselves where he could easily find them.

Violet was the first to spot her brother and began jumping up and down, waving furiously to attract his attention.

Ida Mae said, "Violet, you're not little anymore. Stop all that bouncing around before something falls off."

"She excited, Ida Mae, let her be," said Robert Sr., who began jumping up and down and waving with as much enthusiasm as Violet to get his son's attention.

A smiling Ida Mae shook her head. "Two peas in a pod," she thought, looking at her husband and daughter making a spectacle of themselves.

Spotting Robbie, Ida Mae waved and shouted, *"Over here, son!"*

Chapter 10

Thanksgiving was always a huge affair at the Johnson's home. Ida Mae made the turkey, stuffing, collard greens, and potato salad. Cousin Thelma and her husband Nathaniel arrived bringing two large sweet potato pies. Cousin Ella, her husband James and their son Jimmy, and daughter Valencia came with a ham and big pan of macaroni and cheese. Violet loved Cousin Ella's extra cheesy mac and cheese.

Aunt Sarah came with apple cider and a large pitcher of sweet tea. She was an actress involved with the theater, and an activist. Learning to cook wasn't high on her list of priorities, and after bringing a burnt ham one year, she was discouraged from bringing food to family gatherings.

Violet remembered her mother saying, *"Lord, it don't take nothing to bake a ham. A little glazing, and that's it. You don't even have to glaze the thing, just stick it in the oven to warm and brown a little."* Aunt Sarah had let the ham brown a lot. Ida Mae sliced it up, threw away the burnt meat, and kept the bone for soup. After that, Aunt Sarah was only allowed to bring cider and tea.

Mama and cousins Thelma and Ella made a point of raving over Aunt Sarah's tea, saying, "Sarah, girl, you put your foot in this sweet tea." Aunt Sarah smiled prettily and whispered to Violet, "Store tea. No sense in making something they're going to find fault with."

Violet didn't care that Aunt Sarah couldn't cook. She was impressed with her intellect, artistic talent, and ability to size people up. Violet recalled some of her aunt's most witty comments.

"Ignore him. He's lying through his teeth." "Don't listen to anything that foolish woman says. She enjoys being a doormat. It makes her feel useful." "Stay away from that one. He's going to grow up to be a damn criminal." "He has no good written all over him." "Let's walk over here. She's not right in the head."

Aunt Sarah wanted some alone time with her beloved niece. "Come, show me your new drawings," she said, walking Violet to her bedroom.

"Call us when dinner's ready," Aunt Sarah shouted over her shoulder.

Violet was sure her aunt had some new trinket or forbidden book for her. She was glad her aunt hadn't seen the look Ida Mae gave her as they left the room. She suspected her mother was aware of the books Aunt Sarah gifted her, but chose not to say anything about them. Her mother was always tidying up her room, and she was sure had already come across them.

Though her father wanted to hide the ugly truth about the world from Violet, she knew her mother didn't want her to have any illusions or unrealistic expectations of life, which is why she didn't confront Aunt Sarah about the mature literature.

"I have two new books for you," said Aunt Sarah. "This is a new play by James Baldwin," she said, handing Violet *Blues for Mister Charlie*. "It's emotional, so take a deep breath before you read it. This one is *Selected Poems,* by Gwendolyn Brooks," she said, handing Violet the second book. "Now, show me some of your drawings, so we don't walk out of here as liars," said a smirking Aunt Sarah.

Violet showed her aunt sketches of the butterfly Cecily

caught and told her the story behind it. Aunt Sarah laughed and said she loved Cecily's open-mindedness. The other drawings were of Violet and her friends, and there was also one of Minister X.

Aunt Sarah was impressed by the drawings, especially the one of Malcolm X. "This is how he looked at that rally," she said, awed at the breadth of Violet's talent. She turned and looked deeply into Violet's eyes.

"Without a photo of that day, you captured him flawlessly from memory," she said admiringly.

Violet smiled and nodded shyly.

"You have a special gift of insight, Violet. Never lose that. It'll guide you through life, especially when things get sticky, and trust me, it will."

"Sarah, you and Violet come on, we about to say grace!" yelled Ida Mae.

"Put these away," said Aunt Sarah. "Though I'm sure my sister has already seen the books I've gifted you," she said, shrugging nonchalantly. "Your mama won't say anything because she's got the heart of a rebel. It's just that nobody except me has ever noticed," said Aunt Sarah.

"I've noticed," said Violet.

"Of course, you have, my insightful niece," said Aunt Sarah, squeezing Violet's hand affectionately as they joined their family for Thanksgiving dinner.

Chapter 11

"That sure was a fine meal, ladies," said Cousin James, digging into his teeth with a toothpick and rubbing his round belly.

"Yeah, our wives are great cooks, and Sarah makes a good tea," said Cousin Nathaniel.

Violet giggled and exchanged glances with her cousins Jimmy and Valencia. They knew that cousin Nathaniel walked on eggshells with Aunt Sarah, the one person in the family who pulled no punches putting him in his place when he started bragging about his wealthier lifestyle in front of relatives he knew were struggling. The cousins enjoyed Aunt Sarah's takedowns.

"So, Robbie, tell us how's college life, young man?" asked cousin Nathaniel.

"It's been a great experience, Sir, I've learned a lot," said Robbie.

"And how you like living in that south?" asked Cousin James, who, as he loved saying, "escaped" as soon as he could.

"That's been an experience too," Robbie said with an angry glint in his eye. "The new Civil Rights law hasn't changed many attitudes. It looks like they're going to hang onto segregation as long as they can get away with it, especially since the local law isn't in a rush to enforce it," he said.

"Now that's the south I know," said Cousin James, raising his glass of sweet tea in salute.

"North's got its own issues too," Robert Sr. chimed in.

"I remember my college days," said Cousin Nathaniel changing the subject. He didn't like talking about "that racial stuff," as he often put it. In his opinion, it was time to move on from it.

Cousin James always countered, "Sure Nate, as soon as racists in power allow Negros to move on from it."

Reminiscing, Cousin Nathaniel said, "I ran track in high school and earned myself a college scholarship."

Robert Sr. and Cousin James exchanged a knowing look.

Violet, Valencia, and Jimmy smiled and sat up in their seats, waiting for the fireworks to begin. Cousin Nathaniel told this story every time someone brought up college.

"Running track in college changed my life. I was good, real good, almost made the Olympics too. Great experience," said Cousin Nathaniel.

"Yeah, you got lucky," said Cousin James.

"We make our own luck," Cousin Nathaniel responded smugly.

"Sometimes yes, sometimes, no," retorted Cousin James. "You ran track. Seems you should know about hurdles."

Cousin Ella, stung by the slight, sat up straight and said, "Our babies are going to college." She hated Cousin Nathaniel's need to always put down family. "It's good you got to go to college and didn't have to help your parents sharecrop like the rest of us. We're not all blessed the same," she said, looking at Cousin Thelma.

Violet saw the cloud of sadness cover the eyes of Cousin Thelma who desperately wanted children of her own.

Everyone grew quiet, and then Aunt Sarah, as cheery as ever, said, "Well, I don't have a husband or children, and life has been grand for me! College was fun a long time ago. Honestly, I learned more over the years from traveling and living life. *I say we toast family. Nobody like them in the world!*" she said, downing the entire glass of wine.

Robbie, Violet, Valencia, and Jimmy smiled, enjoying Aunt Sarah's one-upmanship at setting everyone straight.

Chapter 12

Violet was sitting on a chair in Robbie's room, watching him pack for his trip back to college. Her father arranged for him to leave New York in the evening and arrive in Georgia the next day while the sun was still shining. He was taking no chances with his son's safety.

"So, what's college like?" asked Violet.

Robbie said, "It's great, I've enjoyed my time. Don't tell mama and daddy, but I've participated in several protests."

"You some radical now?" asked a smiling Violet. She was happy to know her brother had joined the movement.

"No more than you and Aunt Sarah with your X rallies," said Robbie, giving Violet a teasing smile.

Besides Cecily and Shirley, Robbie was the only other person who knew about Violet's activist spirit. She might not be marching up and down and sitting in, but she fully supported the civil rights movement.

"Aunt Sarah said, sometimes you have to get up in the Devil's face and let him know you're not taking his crap," said Violet.

Robbie laughed and said, "My group aligns more with Dr. King and the peaceful nonviolence marches. Mama and daddy like Dr. King, but if they knew what I was doing, they would be concerned for my safety no matter how righteous the cause," he said.

Violet nodded her agreement.

"I also joined a fraternity," said Robbie, showing Violet his branding.

A shocked Violet stared at Robbie's arm before reaching over and tracing the branding.

"That must have hurt," she said.

"Trust me, it hurt a lot," said Robbie.

"I have to admit, I don't understand or exactly agree with branding," said Violet. "I get the lasting friendships part, which is good, but branding is what they used to do to slaves."

"It's more than that," Robbie said defensively. "It's a brotherhood."

"If you say so," said Violet, not understanding or liking it one bit.

Changing the subject, Robbie said, "Morehouse is great, the south not so much. I'd like you to apply to colleges in the north because once I graduate, you'll be down there with no kin nearby."

"Why?" asked Violet. "Segregation is almost over."

"As I said at Thanksgiving, passing a federal law is one thing, but persuading the local law to abide by it is another. Besides, you're a hothead when it comes to racism, and I'm not sure the south is for you, little sister. All I'm asking is that you keep your options open."

Though Violet was excited about attending Spelman, she decided to heed Robbie's warning.

"I don't like worrying mama and daddy for more money," she said.

Robbie reached for his wallet and handed Violet several bills. "I've been saving up. You don't have to tell them, but for me, please do whatever you can to stay in the north."

Violet knew that Robbie was leaving a lot unsaid. She wondered what happened to put that hard look in his eyes. He had always been quiet and light-hearted, but the south changed him, and she didn't know if it was a good thing or not.

Violet reached over and hugged her brother, planting a kiss on his cheek.

"You're the best brother ever, Robbie. Well, I better let you get ready for your trip back to school."

It was slight, but Violet didn't miss the darkness that clouded Robbie's eyes or the tightening of his mouth as she left his room.

"What the heck is going on in the south?" she wondered.

Chapter 13

December 1964

"I like how that lady snatched that doll screaming, *'It's the last one. I need it for my daughter.'* Only to find out there was a whole wall of the same dolls on the other side," Cecily said, laughing.

"Oh, my goodness, her expression was priceless," said Shirley, giggling.

Violet, also laughing said, "That was a nice end to our Christmas shopping. I love Christmas, but the hysteria over the latest thing is getting out of hand."

The girls were in a joyous holiday mood, hanging out in Violet's living room, where they enjoyed the ham and cheese sandwiches and marshmallow filled hot chocolate her mother made them, while they watched *Carmen Jones* featuring Dorothy Dandridge, Harry Belafonte, Pearl Bailey, and Diahann Carroll on a large black and white Zenith television.

"I love *Carmen Jones*," said Violet.

"It's such a beautiful story," said Cecily, mimicking Dorothy Dandridge's dance moves.

"It's one of my favorites," said Shirley.

"Looks like we're going to have a white Christmas," said Cecily, dancing around the Johnson's Christmas tree. "I do miss Christmas in South Carolina, chopping down our Christmas tree and being around a big family, but having snow makes it feel more like the holidays," she said.

"That's because it's all still new to you," said Violet. "A decade from now, I promise you'll be well over it."

"I can take it or leave it," said Shirley. "We'll be out of school, that's all I care about."

Ida Mae walked into the room looking sullen. "Cecily, your parents need you to come home, dear," she said.

Puzzled, Cecily said, "This early?" It was Saturday and just after 4:00 pm. The three of them usually hung out until at least 6:30 pm on the weekends.

"Yes, sweetheart, they need you. Come, we'll walk you home," Ida Mae said, avoiding eye contact with Cecily. "Shirley, Violet, get your things on so we can walk Cecily," she said.

Cecily asked, "Is everything okay, Mrs. Johnson?" Something was off, but she couldn't figure out what it could be.

"Your parents will discuss it with you, dear."

Violet and Shirley exchanged glances.

Having grown up with Violet, Shirley had come to know her friend's mother well enough to know that something was profoundly wrong.

The girls and Ida Mae walked Cecily home, and as they approached her door, it was immediately pulled open by her father who'd obviously been waiting for his daughter to arrive.

Cecily took one look at him, and her mother standing nearby and knew that something in her life had altered.

"Daddy, mama, what's happened?"

"Cecily," Michael Brooks said, a sob escaping from his throat as he held tightly onto his wife Lillian, who looked ready to collapse, "The Army came and told us Travis was killed, over in Nam."

Cecily's heart-wrenching scream pierced her apartment building.

The Johnsons arrived home from Travis' funeral accompanied by Shirley and her mother Sheila Williams. The two families had supported Cecily and her parents who were still in shock over their loss, even housing some of their kin who'd arrived from the south to attend the funeral.

"It was a lovely funeral," said Ida Mae, putting on a pot of coffee and slicing up a chocolate cake she'd made earlier.

"The military honors were nice," said Robert Sr., who like most people didn't know what to say following someone's funeral. He was feeling guilty for being so grateful that Robbie had avoided the draft and that he and Ida Mae had been able to scrimp up the money to send him to college. It felt like a selfish way to think following the Brooks's loss, but he couldn't imagine losing his only son. He would forever be haunted at the sight of Michael Brooks weeping over his son's casket.

"Here, let me help you with that," Sheila said to Ida Mae. Like the Johnsons, she felt helpless and didn't know what she should be doing.

Violet and Shirley were sitting in her bedroom, neither saying much to the other. Like their parents, they were at a loss at what to do. The girls had rallied around their inconsolable friend and wished they could be with her at this moment, but understood that Cecily needed to be with her parents whose grief was unbearable.

Violet had called Robbie at Morehouse to tell him about Travis's death. The boys had been friends growing up together in the neighborhood, and though they winded up taking different paths after high school, they still maintained contact through their sisters. Robbie had wanted desperately to come home for the funeral, but the family's finances didn't allow for another trip so soon after his Thanksgiving visit.

Robbie said he would visit the Brooks when he came home for the Christmas holiday. His only concern was that his presence so soon after Travis's death might unintentionally upset them, not because he was alive, but because their son who was his age was not.

Shirley was happy when her mother tapped on Violet's door to say she was ready to leave. Travis's death and its aftermath had left her feeling exhausted, and she wanted desperately to crawl into bed and sleep it all away. For as long as she lived, she would forever remember Cecily's ear-piercing, heart-breaking scream upon learning of her brother's death.

The memory gave Shirley chills. As she went to grab her coat and purse, she turned and gave Violet a hug so fierce, Violet thought her ribs would crack, but she knew it was Shirley's way of saying she loved her.

Violet whispered, "I love you too."

On the verge of tears, Shirley grabbed her belongings and left.

Chapter 14

Cecily returned to school the Monday following Travis's funeral. She had missed classes the previous week as her family made the preparations to bury her brother. Though she wasn't emotionally ready, her mother said that she needed to return and catch up on the schoolwork she missed and get back to a sense of normalcy.

"How could things ever be normal again?" she wondered.

For now, Cecily threw herself into her studies and preparing for her upcoming dance audition. She practiced so hard that she went to bed each night completely exhausted. Cecily knew that Violet and Shirley wanted to spend time with her, and though she could have worked in some time for her friends, she just wanted to be to herself for now. Thankfully, they understood and didn't pressure her.

"Do you want to hang out in the schoolyard?" asked Shirley, finishing up her lunch.

"It's cold outside," said Violet. "Let's just stay here until the period ends. I want to start my math homework so that I won't have a lot to do tonight."

Shirley said, "Have you seen Cecily?"

"She was in chemistry class today, but stayed behind to catch up on her assignments, so I didn't get a chance to speak to her. Ms. Berry said she was excused from making up the work since, well, you know," said Violet, trying to avoid mentioning Travis's death, "but Cecily insisted on making it up anyway. I think she needs to keep busy."

Shirley nodded absently, her attention was focused on Johnny Richardson, who had just walked into the cafeteria with a beaming Regina Bolds clutching his arm. The two had become an item while starring in *A Raisin In The Sun,* and Shirley knew that Violet's feelings were hurt over it. She also suspected that Johnny was secretly crushing on Violet, but too intimidated by her intelligence and artistic talent to make his feelings known. Johnny was far from an aware individual. He was too athletically self-absorbed to pay attention to current events or care about what was happening in the larger world. Shirley knew that as a Negro man, he'd come face to face with his reality eventually.

Noticing the lag in Shirley's response, Violet looked up to see Johnny with Regina. Her heart sank as it did whenever she saw the two together. Johnny, who'd been covertly staring at Violet, saw her glance in his direction and immediately drew Regina into an embrace, eliciting a satisfied smile from the young woman.

Violet looked away, Shirley seethed, and for the first time, Johnny felt shame at hurting Violet after witnessing the wounded look on her face.

Chapter 15

Christmas was a quiet affair at the Johnson's this year. The family didn't think it was respectful to do an elaborate celebration when the Brooks were still grieving the loss of their son.

Traditionally, after opening presents and enjoying a nice family breakfast, they'd drive out to Long Island to spend the day with Cousin Thelma and Nathaniel. Ida Mae and Robert Sr. were happy to have a legitimate reason to beg off this year. They'd had their fill of Nathaniel at Thanksgiving. Ida Mae made a small pot roast with carrots and potatoes for her family and an apple pie for dessert.

Robbie who came home for the holidays was in the living room with his father where they'd spent the day watching sports.

Immediately after arriving home from college, he made the dreaded trek to the Brooks's house to offer his condolences, taking along a pound cake his mother had baked for them. To his surprise, they welcomed him with open arms, happy to have someone so familiar with Travis sing their son's praises. The truth was that Travis was a good guy. He was just one of the unlucky ones getting called up for the draft. "Could easily have been me," thought Robbie.

He was happy to be home and even happier to have a home-cooked meal because his mother was a terrific cook.

He'd enjoyed her pot roast so much he ate seconds and was thinking of going back for thirds. Laverne was also a good cook, but with school, work, and the rallies, she had little time to prepare a home-cooked meal for them.

Robbie was thinking about how best to bring up Laverne, who told him it was time to introduce her to his parents and that she resented spending the holidays without him. He met Laverne his first semester at college, and the two became fast friends and soon after a couple. She attended Spelman and though they were the same age, she was in her senior year having skipped a grade in intermediate school.

Laverne Frazier was from a politically-connected Atlanta Black bourgeoisie family. She already had a job awaiting her with a well-known civil rights attorney and would begin after graduating in the spring and before attending law school in the fall.

Her parents didn't initially think Robbie was the right person for their daughter. He came from a working-class family in the north and lacked the proper connections favored by bougie Negros in the south, but Robbie's intellect and out-standing grades soon changed their mind. Her father Melvin saw promise in him and believed that with his guidance, Robbie would flourish.

Robbie spent more time at Laverne's apartment than he did at the dorm and only stayed there occasionally because he felt guilty about the tuition his hardworking parents were paying. He made a promise to himself that he'd pay them back and then some in the future.

Sick of spending the holidays alone, Laverne gave him an ultimatum when he returned after Thanksgiving break. She said, "Tell your parents about us or move on. I will not continue to be a secret from your family."

After a few days of contemplation, he decided she was right. He approached her father about marrying his daughter and, after getting Melvin Frazier's approval, he presented her with a ring for Christmas. They would marry after he graduated and began his job at Morehouse, a position arranged by Melvin. Now he had to introduce her to his parents.

Taking a deep breath, he said, "Mama, daddy, I need to tell you something."

Chapter 16

"Married?" said Ida Mae and Robert Sr. in unison. Violet stood stock still. She was as much in shock as her parents. She had never thought of her brother as the settling down, getting married type.

"He'd grown in more ways than I'd realized," thought Violet.

"Son, you're about to graduate college, you should be thinking about a career and sowing your oats a little before..."

Robert Sr. trailed off, seeing the look on his wife's face.

"I don't know about sowing nothing other than those work pants of yours," said Ida Mae, throwing daggers at her husband, "but I do know you are too young for marriage," she said to Robbie.

"Mama, you and daddy got married at seventeen," said Robbie in protest.

"Those were different times. Folks didn't have much choice back then but to marry up," said Ida Mae, who earned her own look from her husband.

Robert Sr. said, "So you had no choice. Is that what you're saying, Ida Mae?"

"That's not what I meant, and you know it. Life was harder back then," said Ida Mae

"So, you married me out of necessity and not love?" asked Robert Sr.

"Of course, I loved you. It just made life easier to be married. Violet will have more options," said Ida Mae.

Robert Sr. getting worked up said, "Oh, so if you had more options, you wouldn't have married me?"

"Of course, I would have married you man. Have you heard nothing I said?"

"Oh, I've heard you plenty, Ida Mae."

Violet watched the back and forth between her parents like she was watching a tennis match. She found the exchange comical. "Sure hope it doesn't turn into a full-blown argument," she thought with amusement.

Robbie tried to turn the focus back to him and Laverne before things got out of hand with his parents.

"Mama, daddy, can we calmly discuss Laverne and me?"

"You obviously didn't hear me good since your mouth is all balled up like you fixing to pop husband."

"You're the one who said you only married me cause times was hard," said a pouting Robert Sr.

"Don't put words in my mouth, husband," Ida Mae said tightly.

"I'm going by the ones that done come out of your mouth, wife," retorted Robert Sr.

"Mama, daddy, Laverne and I will just send you an invitation," Robbie said, walking out of the living room and shutting his bedroom door with a loud thud.

"Make sure that Laverne's marrying you for love, son, and not out of necessity!" shouted Robert Sr., earning him a cut eye and teeth sucking from Ida Mae.

Chapter 17

January 1965

"I never thought I'd be happy for the holidays to be over, but I am," said Cecily. "I don't know if I'll ever celebrate it with joy again."

"You will in time," said Violet. "Travis will always be in your heart and on your mind, but you have to keep moving forward."

"Violet, please thank your mother for the pound cake," said Cecily. "It came in handy with the spaghetti mama whipped up. It was all she could manage," she said sadly. "Mama spent most of the day in bed, and daddy was looking at sports, more than actually watching it. I stayed in my room reading and practicing for today."

"Me and mama had a quiet Christmas," said Shirley. "We weren't in the mood for celebrating much this year. We stayed home, roasted a small chicken, and made mashed potatoes and peas. By 3 pm, we were in our pajamas drinking hot chocolate. It was that kind of Christmas this year."

"It was mostly uneventful at my house too," said Violet, recalling her day and the hilarity that ensued with her parents. She decided not to mention Robbie getting married because she felt it would be adding salt to Cecily and her parents' already wounded hearts.

Violet and Shirley accompanied Cecily to her dance

audition. Cecily, dressed in a white leotard, tights, tutu skirt, and silk ballet slippers, chose *Duet & Finale* from the soundtrack of the *Carmen Jones* musical for her performance. She decided on the song because she loved the movie and watching it with her friends was her last moment of peace before the news of Travis's death sent her world hurtling.

Violet and Shirley sat mesmerized as Cecily glided across the dance floor. They'd seen her dance many times, but until that moment had no idea the breadth of her talent. She was pure majesty.

Cecily's friends and the judges faded away, lost was she to the dance. As *Harry Belafonte* sang with pleading desperation of his love for *Carmen,* Cecily's pain over the loss of her brother showed in every leap and dip. When *Dorothy Dandridge* sang of her desire for freedom, Cecily twirled as though fleeing from the arms of torment, her facial expression a look of determination. The dizzying array of emotions was fascinating. Her heart-stopping finale, Carmen's murder scene, saw Cecily in a jeté leap before collapsing, head down, to roaring applause and chants of *Bravo!*

After Cecily's performance, she met with the judges, who said they were looking to make an immediate decision on which dancers would join the troupe.

The moment she was free, Violet and Shirley engulfed her. "You were fabulous!" shouted Violet. "You brought tears to my eyes," said Shirley, dabbing at her eyes.

"I hope the judges thought it was flawless," said Cecily. "The troupe will begin traveling shortly after graduation, and I really want this. Home is so depressing these days, I need a change of scenery!" she said. She hadn't meant to say the last part with such force, but it was the truth.

Violet and Shirley suspected as much. They had noticed

the circles around Cecily's eyes and the rapid weight loss which they knew was the result of her not eating. With her mother despondent and unable to cook, Cecily and her father were fending for themselves. Ida Mae had recently sent food over to the Brooks's house after Violet mentioned Cecily's weight loss. Her mother said that Cecily's mother might need "help" to cope with her loss.

"They would be crazy not to pick you," said Violet with conviction.

"I agree with Violet. You're way too talented to pass on," said Shirley.

"Come on, let's go get burgers and a milkshake, my treat," said Violet. "I'm sure you've worked up an appetite." Her parents had given her extra money. They wanted to make sure that Cecily ate today.

Chapter 18

February 1965

"Oh no! Lord, keep us near the cross!" screamed Ida Mae. *"Who would do such a horrible thing?"*

Robert Sr. was pacing back and forth, saying, *"This just can't be! They took Garvey, killed Kennedy, now Malcolm! This just ain't right!"*

Violet's parents were in the living room watching the evening news when they heard of the assassination of Malcolm X.

Violet bolted out of her bedroom at the sound of their shouting. *"Mama and daddy, what's happened?"*

"They done killed Malcolm X, that's what!" shouted Robert Sr.

Violet thought maybe she heard incorrectly. "Malcolm X is dead? No, that can't be, and when did her parents start liking Minister X anyway?"

Violet turned slowly towards the television news showing the chaos at the Audubon Ballroom, people shouting on the streets, and an official saying that Malcolm X had been shot multiple times and was pronounced dead at 3:30 pm at Columbia Presbyterian Hospital.

"Malcolm X, whose brash takedown of the establishment that continually oppressed Negros, is dead," thought Violet.

Just then, the big canary yellow rotary phone on the

kitchen wall, with the long cord that snaked around the house, rang. Violet knew it was her aunt calling to find out if she'd heard the news.

Violet stood up and calmly walked out of the living room, past the ringing phone, and taking hold of her bedroom door, slammed it with such force that Robert Sr. and Ida Mae jumped. They were too stunned to move. Never before had their daughter acted in such a way.

"Will we never win?!" screamed Violet.

The ringing phone went unanswered.

Days after learning the shocking news of the assassination of Malcolm X, Aunt Sarah, Shirley, and Cecily rallied around Violet, knowing how crushed she was over the civil rights leader's death.

It wasn't until after his death that Robert Sr. and Ida Mae learned about their daughter attending the minister's rallies. They knew she had strong political opinions because she often shared them, and they would beam at her intelligence, but never once did they think she was attending his rallies.

The news reported on Martin Luther King's Western Union to Malcolm X's widow, Betty Shabazz. It said, *"While we did not always see eye to eye on methods to solve the race problem, I always had a deep affection for Malcolm and felt that he had the great ability to put his finger on the existence and root of the problem."*

Robert Sr. gave Aunt Sarah a tongue lashing for, as he said, "Involving Violet in such matters."

Sarah stared on, allowing him to purge, before asking, "Do you honestly believe that I dragged Violet to those rallies, you foolish man? I accompanied her to make sure she was clear on the proper, peaceful way to protest. It's time you and Ida Mae stop burying your head in the sand. Violet's not a child anymore. She is a young woman, with strong opinions and views learned through reading and research, not brainwashing. Trust me, she's no one's fool, dear. Sorry you're late to her party, but she is who she is. Besides, Malcolm X's rallies were far more peaceful than those rallies taking place in the south. Now, I came to see my niece, not you two," said Sarah, sauntering down to Violet's room, having the last word as usual.

Chapter 19

"I don't understand why there is so much cruelty in the world," said Violet. "I mean what's it all for if only some people get to be free and live happily?"

"My mama said jealousy and fear breed contempt," said Shirley. "Malcolm X was strong, fearless, and unafraid to speak his mind."

"That's why you have to live each day doing what brings you joy and avoid unhappiness," said Cecily. "There are no guarantees."

To Violet, Cecily sounded idealistic, out of touch with reality, and as usual, escaping into her world of make-believe when things got tough. Violet knew it was why Cecily loved dancing so much. She enjoyed the fantasy of it all.

"Well, I don't believe in masking truths," thought Violet.

"God didn't create this world for some people only. I'll never stop fighting for my rights," said Violet.

"All we do is fight," said Cecily sullenly.

"We fight and endure, just like the ancestors," said Shirley. "My mama endured after my father died, her sharecropping parents endured, and so did all the others before them, that's why I'm here, to tell their story of endurance. It's what we've always done."

"Yeah, well, I'm sick of enduring, I plan to thrive," said Violet.

Chapter 20

March 1965

"Hello, may I please speak to Cecily Brooks?"

"This is Cecily Brooks."

"Hello Cecily, this is Anabelle Gibson from Show Stoppers calling about your audition."

Cecily's heart stopped. She had been waiting to hear from them for weeks. They took so long that she assumed she didn't win a spot in the troupe. "Good news or bad, this is it," she thought. She crossed her fingers and waited to hear the decision.

"Sorry it's taken us so long to get back to you. We've had a bevy of dancers to weigh through. Weeding through the bad talent was easy," laughed Anabelle, "but it takes time to make a decision when there's so much good talent, and remarkably, there was a lot of good talent."

"No sense in prolonging what I'm sure has been an agonizing two months. Hopefully, you're still available and interested because we'd love for you to join our troupe and become a Show Stopper."

Cecily thought she'd pass out and be unable to say yes. Taking a deep breath and putting on her best professional voice, she said, "I am truly honored to be picked. Yes, I'd love to become a Show Stopper."

"That's great to hear. Now, let's discuss particulars," said Annabelle.

Cecily was over the moon.

Chapter 21

"Let's raise our sodas to Cecily," said Aunt Sarah who took the girls to an Italian restaurant that she and her theater friends frequented in the Village that was friendly to Negros. They were celebrating Cecily winning a spot in the dance troupe.

"To all of your hard work and dedication," said Aunt Sarah.

"To never giving up," said Shirley.

"To going after what you want, regardless of the odds, and winning," said Violet.

"To Cecily," they said in unison.

With all the turmoil around them, Aunt Sarah wanted to take the girls somewhere outside their daily surroundings.

First, there were last summer's Harlem riots resulting from the police shooting and killing of 15-year-old James Powell. Then last month Malcolm X was assassinated and earlier this month another march in Harlem, protesting that bloody Sunday in Selma, Alabama. It's one tragedy after another for Negroes.

Aunt Sarah was one of the few adults in their lives brave enough to venture beyond racially constructed walls. No one kept Aunt Sarah in a box.

She also wanted to do something special for Cecily after everything the young woman had been through with the loss of her brother and after learning about her mother's emotional breakdown.

"Poor thing can't get past her grief," Aunt Sarah said to Violet. "Such a shame she's missing out on her daughter's achievements."

She wished Cecily had opted to attend college, but was happy that her dancing talent was opening doors for her. Aunt Sarah didn't want to alarm Violet, but she was concerned about Cecily traveling with a troupe across the country. She would reach out to friends in the industry to keep watch over the impressionable young woman.

Aunt Sarah glanced from one girl to the other as they talked animatedly among themselves. "Each one beautiful, talented and unique in her own way," she thought with a smile.

"I'd like to raise my glass to all of you," she said.

"I thought we were celebrating Cecily?" asked Shirley

"Yes, we are," said Aunt Sarah, "but I'm leaving soon. The theater calls darlings, and sadly I won't be back in time for your graduation."

"Oh, no!" said Violet.

She knew Violet would be disappointed, but this was the life she had chosen and loved.

"Sorry love, Aunt Sarah goes where the show goes. Something tells me one day soon you'll understand," she said, smiling.

Unlike Ida Mae and Robert Sr., she didn't believe Violet was destined to work in some stuffy old law firm. She'd watched her niece since she was in pampers and saw what everyone, including Violet failed to see. Violet was artsy and had way too much passion and talent to be stuck in an office.

"Ida Mae might have raised you, but you'll always be my daughter," thought Aunt Sarah, looking at Violet adoringly.

Raising her glass for another toast, Aunt Sarah said, "You ladies are butterflies. Now you go out into that big bad world, flap your beautiful, glorious wings and show everyone what true beauty and talent looks like. To my butterflies. *Fly!*"

Chapter 22

"It was so nice of your aunt to take us to dinner," said Shirley.

"You're lucky to have an aunt like her. She's so worldly and knowledgeable," said Cecily. "I'm grateful for all the tips she gave me for traveling with the troupe."

"Aunt Sarah is very special to me," said Violet. "She's open and honest, and I've learned so much from her. I'm disappointed that she won't be attending our graduation. It won't be the same without her."

"True, but she got you a part in that play, and I'm sure she'll come back to see your performance," said Shirley.

"Most likely, but I never dreamed she wouldn't be around to see me graduate. I owe this achievement to her as much as mama and daddy," said Violet.

"Performing is in her blood, and like she said, she goes where the show goes," said Cecily.

"Cheer up, time to shop for prom dresses. What color are you two wearing?" asked Shirley.

Violet said, "Hmm, I'm thinking of wearing..."

"*Violet!*" Cecily and Shirley said in unison.

Violet smiled and said, "How'd you guess?"

Chapter 23

April 1965

"I'm happy the two of you will be together at Spelman," said Cecily.

"You should have applied so that we'd all be together," said Shirley. She was still upset at Cecily for choosing not to attend college. Shirley thought her friend was making a mistake and hoped that her talent would sustain her.

Cecily's father had also been disappointed that she wasn't going to college, but after losing his son and his wife, by the looks of it, he was happy that she had somewhere to land.

Violet was more understanding, but like Shirley, she too worried about Cecily's future should dancing fail to work out.

The girls were in Violet's bedroom getting ready for the prom.

"We still have time together before I leave," said Cecily, staring in the mirror, twisting her hair into her signature ballerina updo. She looked spectacular in a long baby blue prom dress and long matching gloves. For contrast, she wore silky white heels and faux diamond drop earrings. The outfit was her homage to Dorothy Dandridge, and the *Carmen Jones* soundtrack that she believed set her on her career path.

Violet wore a knee-length, cinched waist, flared violet dress that revealed her lovely legs. The color was heavenly against her smooth pecan brown skin. Her shoes were silver and paired with a matching clutch purse. Violet's shoulder-length hair was styled in big bouncy curls and her jewelry comprised a thin silver bracelet and large silver hoop earrings that gave the dressy outfit an edgy look.

Shirley had on a long A-line two-tone, silver and black dress. The top portion was silver with black lace, while the bottom was satiny silver. She styled her hair in an afro puff upswept with a sparkly band. On her feet were leather slingback heels and falling from her left shoulder was a long-strapped, small, rounded leather purse. Her ears sparkled with her mother's stud earrings, a fifth-anniversary gift from Shirley's father. It meant a lot to Shirley to have a part of her father since he couldn't be there to share her special night. Her only other jewelry was a vintage silver watch that no longer told the time but was passed down from her grandmother, a wedding gift from Shirley's grandfather to his new bride. She felt embraced by ancestors.

Chapter 24

The prom, held at a local banquet hall, was decorated in black, red, green, and gold. On the left side of the entryway was a banner welcoming and congratulating the Harlem High School Class of 1965.

The room was electric, sparkling with the excited energy of the senior class, who were reliving memorable moments shared with their classmates. Many of the students had grown up together making it a bittersweet evening, knowing the ties that had bound them together since youth would soon loosen as they moved onto the next chapter of their lives.

Trent was Shirley's date, and after presenting her with a beautiful white corsage kissed her intimately, surprising Violet and Cecily, who didn't know the two had reached that level of intimacy.

Martin, who'd spent the school year discussing assignments and grades but too shy to approach Cecily for a date, got up the nerve and asked her to the prom. He was pleasantly surprised when she agreed. Soon after, he sought Violet's help in picking out a corsage, and together they chose a small, baby blue and white wristlet. Violet was all too happy to assist him. "Heaven forbid he should ruin Cecily's dramatic *Carmen Jones* look," she thought with a smile.

Violet, unable to pin down Johnny, accepted an invitation from Clinton Daniels, the class valedictorian. Clinton was tall and stocky, and though his demeanor was serious, he had a friendly personality. They had known each other since elementary school and had a friendly rapport. The couples were having a great time, laughing, taking pictures, and dancing to the sounds of Motown.

Johnny, who recently broke up with Regina, came dateless. The thought of asking Violet to the prom never entered into his ego-driven mind. He just assumed she would be dateless, allowing him the chance to get close to her.

Johnny was surprised and annoyed after arriving and finding her with Clinton, the smartest teen in school, adding to his insecurities. Making matters worse, Martin and Trent, each smitten with their dates, brushed him off when he tried to finagle his way into their group. Johnny couldn't take his eyes off Violet, who looked stunning in her violet dress. Unfortunately for him, her feelings had begun to cool, having grown tired of his elusive, childish behavior.

Violet was laughing and congratulating some of the seniors on the decorating committee when Johnny sidled up to her and pleadingly asked, "Will you save me a dance, Violet?"

"We'll see," she said nonchalantly, as Clinton walked up behind Johnny and led Violet to the dance floor, pulling her in close for a slow dance. Clinton's actions took both Violet and Johnny by surprise. The aggressive move made Violet give him a second look.

It was a magical evening for the class of 1965.

Chapter 25

May 1965

"I can't believe we only have one month left," said Violet. "Next month, this time, we will officially be college freshmen."

"You'll be a college freshman, and I will be a professional dancer," said a gleeful Cecily.

Violet smiled. Cecily was slowly returning to her cheery, optimistic self.

"The last thing I should be doing before joining the dance troupe is putting on pounds, but I think we should hit all of the neighborhood spots before we fade into the future," said Cecily. "I have a taste for barbeque from that greasy spoon on Lenox."

"I'm sure I can get chicken and waffles in the south, but it won't be the same as eating it in Harlem," said Violet.

"Chicken and waffles sound good, or maybe salmon croquettes and grits," said Cecily unable to make up her mind. "Daddy was eating at the greasy spoon while mama recuperated. She's cooking more these days and finally went back to work. I think she's going to be okay in time."

"She called mama the other day to thank her for helping with food and all," said Violet. "Mama said she sounded better than she had in a while."

Cecily was happy that her mother was making progress. She was still worried about leaving her, but dancing with the troupe was her dream come true. She couldn't give up this chance. It might be her only shot to prove herself.

"What about you, Shirley? Where do you want to eat before we leave?" asked Violet.

Violet and Shirley had received acceptance letters from Spelman. "Dormmates!" they had screamed.

Cecily gave Shirley a perplexed look, "Hey girl, food, eat?" she said, mimicking eating.

"I don't feel well. I can't think about food right now," said Shirley.

"The greasy spoon has soup," said Violet.

"Sure do, their homemade chicken soup is delicious," said Cecily, chiming in.

"I don't want any soup," snapped Shirley.

Startled, Cecily asked, "What's wrong, Shirley? You've been acting weird lately."

"Senior ditch day and graduation are coming up. Then, we'll be on summer vacation before heading to Spelman. You should be excited," said Violet.

"I don't feel so good. I'm going home to lie down. See you later," said Shirley, beating a hasty retreat.

"Feel better," said Violet, distracted by the exciting news she'd been dying to tell her friends.

"I'll call you later," said Cecily, giving Shirley a quizzical look as she left.

"I have something to tell you. I wanted to tell Shirley, but I'm not sure she would approve. She's so freaking straight and narrow about everything," said Violet.

"Hmmm," Cecily said skeptically.

"I have a summer job," blurted out Violet.

Cecily said, "Doing what, flipping burgers?"

"Nope," said Violet, displaying a wide smile.

"Well, what other kind of job is there?" asked Cecily.

"Acting in a play and learning set designing," said Violet.

This time Cecily turned her quizzical gaze on Violet.

"What?"

"Aunt Sarah had me audition for a part in an off-Broadway play and I got it—for the summer anyway. It's a small part, but I'll have the chance to put my artistic talent to work learning set designing too," she said excitedly.

Cecily smiled and said, "Congratulations! You've been bitten by the acting bug!"

"I have," said Violet. "I didn't see this coming, but I think it's something I want to pursue. I haven't given up on becoming a civil rights attorney, but I love acting, just losing myself into a character."

"Now, who's idealistic?" asked Cecily. "Welcome to the world of performing."

Violet beamed.

Chapter 26

"This is a nightmare. How could this be? We used protection. I was careful each time, mama, I swear."

"No protection is 100% foolproof," said a stoic Sheila Williams, who couldn't bring herself to look at Shirley. "How ironic," she thought. She'd always thought her smart, responsible daughter was 100% foolproof.

Shirley and her mother were standing outside the doctor's office where'd they'd gone for the pregnancy test. Shirley had never been late since she began getting her menstruation, so when her time came and went, she knew for certain that she was pregnant, but waited two weeks to be sure, then steeled herself and told her mother what she suspected.

Sheila had been floored, but hopeful to the end that it wasn't true. After they received the results, she wanted to scream, *"How could you be so stupid? You should have known better! How could you do this to us? You know we can't afford another mouth to feed."* Then came another gut punch from Shirley.

"I'm sorry, mama, but I can't keep it. I know you think it's wrong, but I don't want to be a mother, not now. I'm not ready for this."

Shirley had decided not to tell Violet and Cecily. Some things were just too personal to share with anyone, and she had to admit that she was ashamed after so often berating them about morality and then herself falling short.

"Mama, I've made up my mind," said a resolute Shirley.

Sheila refused to look at her daughter, but said, "I know a doctor who handles these types of situations. I don't want you to think I approve of this, Shirley, because I do not."

"It's not about approving mama. Like you said, we can't afford another mouth to feed, and I have too much that I want to do. I'm so sorry, but I can't have a baby right now and most certainly not for Trent Jones."

There was so much that Sheila wanted to hurl at Shirley. She was disappointed and not at all pleased with having to help with such a thing, but Shirley wasn't a child anymore. She was a young woman, and this decision was hers to make. Regardless of how angry she was, Shirley was still her daughter, and she didn't want her life ruined.

"I'll make the arrangements," said Sheila.

Chapter 27

Cecily asked Violet, "Do you know what's wrong with Shirley?"

"She's sick," said Violet, distractedly reading her lines for the off-Broadway play.

Cecily said, "Do you believe her?"

"She's been throwing up a lot lately, so she must be," said Violet.

"Or pregnant," said Cecily.

Violet looked up. The thought of Shirley being pregnant never entered her mind.

"She couldn't be, could she?" asked a horrified Violet.

"It could be the reason she's been so distant lately," said Cecily.

"Shirley has been distant lately," thought Violet. "I've been so wrapped up in end-of-the-term activities and preparing for the play that I didn't notice that my best friend might be going through something."

"I've been neglecting Cecily too," Violet thought with remorse. "Even though she loves dancing, she's trying to escape her pain. Some friend I've been."

"We should go see her," said Violet.

"No," said Cecily. "If Shirley isn't sharing this with us, then she doesn't want anyone to know, and we need to respect her privacy," she said.

Violet wanted desperately to drag the truth out of Shirley, but knew that Cecily was right.

"I wonder what she's going to do," said Violet.

"Have the baby. What else she can she do?" asked Cecily.

"There's something else she could do," said Violet. "There are people who could help her with it."

"That's a horrible thought. It's not the baby's fault!" said Cecily.

"I know what I'd do if it were me," said Violet adamantly.

"It's not what I'd do," said Cecily with conviction.

Violet said, "Well, it's a good thing we don't have to make that decision."

"But Shirley does," said Cecily.

"And she'll make the decision that's right for her," said Violet, putting an end to the conversation.

Chapter 28

"Here, sip this," said Sheila. "How do you feel?"

"Tired, a little nauseous, and I have cramps."

A weary Sheila Williams nodded. She wanted to put this whole episode behind them.

"Rest. I'll check on you later."

Shirley lay in the darkened room, contemplating the last several weeks. It all felt like an out-of-body experience. "How did I get here?" she wondered. After finding out that she was pregnant, she refused to speak to Trent. Deep down, she knew it wasn't his fault alone, but the shock had clouded her thoughts. Even worse, she had avoided her friends.

She knew Violet would understand her decision, but wasn't sure that Cecily would. Cecily believed deeply in nature and life.

Shirley who'd always been a firm believer in women's rights knew that this choice was hers and hers alone to make. Still, she hated having had to make it.

Shirley wept until she was drained and then drifted off into a deep sleep.

Chapter 29

June 1965

"Are you feeling better?" Asked Violet.

"Getting there," Shirley said hesitantly.

Taking a deep breath, she said, "I have to tell you something."

Violet and Cecily exchanged glances.

Cecily said, "No, you don't." She knew Shirley was greatly affected by her decision. "You made your choice, and it's time to move on," she said giving, Shirley an out on explaining her actions.

"I agree," said Violet, proud of the way Cecily was handling the situation. Though Cecily disagreed with Shirley's decision, she loved her friend enough not to cause her more pain.

Shirley teared up and nodded. Her friends knew her secret and chose to respect her privacy.

"Are you up for senior skip day?" asked Violet.

Shirley said, "Yeah, school's almost over. I don't want to miss out on anything."

"Then grab your skates and let's go," said Cecily.

"Afterwards, let's go for chicken and waffles," said Shirley.

The senior class turned out in force at the skating rink for senior skip day. The students skated around the roller rink, spinning and showing off their impressive dance moves.

Twirling and dancing like she was on stage, Cecily said, "Wouldn't it be nice if there was a show that played Negro music and showed off our dance moves?"

"I'd love to see that," said Violet.

Shirley was dancing and genuinely enjoying herself for the first time since prom night when Trent skated by, smiling, and giving her a puzzled look.

She gave him a half-smile and then turned away. After graduation, they would be heading in totally different directions. She was off to college, and he to work with his uncle as a long-distance truck driver. Shirley cared deeply for Trent, but knew that it was time to put that chapter of her life behind her and move forward.

Violet and Cecily saw the brief exchange, and the sadness that came over Shirley.

Violet said, "This was fun, but I'm hungry. Chicken and waffles?"

Shirley's eyes shined with unshed tears as she nodded her agreement.

Chapter 30

"Always remember that you are capable of greatness! And so, class of 1965, go forth and do amazing things!" said Clinton Daniels, the class valedictorian.

The students tossed their caps high in the air, happy and exuberant at completing the first chapter of their young lives.

The girls gathered outside the auditorium hugging and congratulating classmates and taking pictures with their families.

"I'm so proud of you," said Robert Sr. embracing Violet. *"My baby girl got her diploma and is off to college,"* he said, beaming with pride.

"Congratulations, little sister," Robbie said to Violet, enveloping her in a big hug.

"Thanks, Robbie. I wish Aunt Sarah could be here."

"She is," said Ida Mae, hugging Violet and handing her an envelope and small blue box. "Sarah told me to give this to you the moment you got your diploma."

"Hold this for me, mama," said Violet, handing Ida Mae her diploma.

Ida Mae put the diploma in her purse, giving the bag a tap, like she was tucking away a winning number slip.

Violet read the note in the envelope that said simply, "I love you. Fly." As she opened the blue box, Shirley, Cecily, and their families walked over.

"*How beautiful,*" exclaimed Violet, holding up a necklace of a violet butterfly.

"Here, I'll help you put it on," said Shirley.

The families exchanged greetings, congratulating the girls on their achievement.

Ida Mae caught the sad look that passed over Lillian Brooks's face as she glanced at Robbie and walked towards her offering a cheery smile. Ida Mae knew things would never be the same for Lillian, but she'd find a way to cope in time. She said a silent prayer for her.

Trying to keep the happy momentum going, Ida Mae said, "*Y'all come on, I got food ready at the house.*"

Chapter 31

"This is the last time we'll all be together for a long while," said Violet.

The friends were experiencing the bittersweet emotions that came from the evolving shifts in life.

"You and Shirley will be together in the fall," said Cecily.

"Yes, but you won't be with us," said Shirley sullenly. "Things won't ever be like this again."

Cecily smiled and said, "You two had each other long before I became the third wheel."

"Three wheels are closer to a whole car than two," said Violet. "We have a bond and will always be best friends. Nothing will ever change that."

The girls came together in a group hug, promising to be *"Friends for life!"*

"We better get to Regina's party," said Cecily.

"Wait," said Violet, grabbing her Polaroid camera. "We'll take pictures with the class later, but this one is just for us." Raising the camera, she said, *"1, 2, 3 cheese!"*

Chapter 32

The girls arrived at Regina's party at the community center dressed in varying styles of blue jeans, black blouses, and black pumps.

Silver, gold, and white balloons and streamers decorated the center. A large blown-up photo of the senior class, along with their yearbook, sat on a table near a whiteboard, where the seniors wrote their names and left encouraging messages for the future. Regina planned to save it for future class reunions.

The students enjoyed the refreshments, danced, mingled, and swapped stories about their four years of high school and plans for the future.

"Your speech was great," Violet said to Clinton, who planted himself at her side the moment she arrived at the party.

"Thank you, I was nervous but shook it off and got into a groove," said Clinton.

Violet understood, having experienced the same feelings when she was acting.

"I'm going to miss you, Violet. I hope we stay in touch," he said earnestly.

Violet smiled and said, "I'd like that." She was coming to care for Clinton, though she wasn't sure how they would manage a long-distance relationship with him attending Howard in Washington and her at Spelman in Georgia.

Violet and her friends were laughing and reminiscing when Regina walked over.

"Thank you so much for putting everything together for us," said Cecily. "The decorations are beautiful."

"You did a great job," said Shirley. "I took a lot of pictures so that I will always remember this night."

Regina beamed. She worked tirelessly to make the senior class's last time together memorable and was happy to receive all the glowing praise. Regina loved planning things and picking out decor and wondered if a career as a party planner was in her future. She knew her parents would never support her endeavor because when she mentioned taking acting classes after starring in *A Raisin In The Sun,* her father laughed and tut-tutted the idea, deflating her hopes of pursuing acting.

"How ironic that my dreams were being dashed like Beneatha's," thought Regina. Her father considered teaching a respectable career for women who chose not to be what they were "bred" to be—housewives.

Regina didn't doubt that teaching could be a rewarding career, but she wanted so much more. Why shouldn't she be able to push boundaries?

"Can I speak to you for a minute, Violet?" asked Regina.

Violet was surprised at the request. She and Regina had never been particularly close, even less so when she began dating Johnny, piquing Violet's jealousy.

"Umm, sure," said Violet.

Shirley and Cecily stared on, surprised that Johnny's ex-girlfriend wanted to speak privately with Violet.

"I'm glad you came," said Regina.

"Me too, it's a great party," said Violet.

Getting to the point, Regina said, "I heard through the grapevine that you and Johnny have feelings for each other."

Violet was shocked at Regina's boldness.

"I used to like Johnny, Regina, but I'm over it. It wouldn't have worked out anyway, with me headed in one direction and him in another. I'm sorry that you two broke up."

Regina gave Violet a dubious, knowing look and said, "Sorry about as much as I am. I'm so over him, too. I could tell he liked you because he talked about you way too much."

That bit of news both shocked and gave Violet a hint of pleasure. "His loss," she said, smiling.

"Yup, we both are," said Regina. "You didn't miss out on anything with him. Johnny is a shallow person."

None of what Regina said was new or surprising. Wanting to put all talk of Johnny to a rest, Violet smiled politely and said, "I wish you the best Regina. I can't wait to see what you plan for our ten-year reunion."

Regina displayed a 100-watt smile. "Maybe teaching will help fund the career I want," she thought, already plotting how to get from under her parent's financial thumb.

The moment Violet walked back over to her friends, Cecily, bursting for news, said, "What was that about?"

Just then, Johnny walked in, and they turned to look at him.

"Nothing important," said Violet, staring at the boy who had held her interest for four years, but no more.

"No time for looking back," she said. *"It's time to spread our wings and soar!"*

Butterflies

Butterflies are not meant to live in glass jars

Trapped,

With punctured tops

And seepings of air to breathe.

Would that they could be moths,

Undesirable

Free to flutter in the sunshine and breeze

Unbothered.

But, alas, butterflies were not meant to be moths,

But Butterflies,

Able to spread their wings.

A beauty for all the world to behold.

To survive the butterfly must learn to

Fly high

Fly far,

Fly free.

Citations

12 Surprising Facts about Tiger Swallowtails (Butterfly Gardening 101). https://butterflygardening101.com/fascinating-tiger-swallowtail-facts/

Exchange between Beneatha and Asagai, excerpted from Lorraine Hansberry's *A Raisin In The Sun.*

"This is the telegram MLK sent Malcolm X's wife after her husband's assassination" (Phil Edwards, Vox.com, 21 Feb. 2015).

Author's Note & Acknowledgements

Butterflies began as an English essay assignment but along the way became a labor of love. I hope you've enjoyed getting to know each of the characters as I did in writing their stories.

I wish to give special thanks to Professor "Dr. J" for introducing me to my true passion—writing. I would also like to give thanks to everyone at Atmosphere Press involved with helping me achieve my dream of becoming a published author.

Special thanks to Ms. Angelou and Ms. Morrison.

Most of all, I'd like to thank my true loves Cameron, Derick, Matt, and Isabel – Family.

About Atmosphere Press

Atmosphere Press is an independent, full-service publisher for excellent books in all genres and for all audiences. Learn more about what we do at atmospherepress.com.

We encourage you to check out some of Atmosphere's latest releases, which are available at Amazon.com and via order from your local bookstore:

The Friendship Quilts, a novel by June Calender

Nine Days, a novel by Judy Lannon

Shadows of Robyst, a novel by K. E. Maroudas

Home Within a Landscape, a novel by Alexey L. Kovalev

Motherhood, a novel by Siamak Vakili

Death, The Pharmacist, a novel by D. Ike Horst

Mystery of the Lost Years, a novel by Bobby J. Bixler

Bone Deep Bonds, a novel by B. G. Arnold

Terriers in the Jungle, a novel by Georja Umano

Into the Emerald Dream, a novel by Autumn Allen

His Name Was Ellis, a novel by Joseph Libonati

The Cup, a novel by D. P. Hardwick

The Empathy Academy, a novel by Dustin Grinnell

Tholocco's Wake, a novel by W. W. VanOverbeke

Dying to Live, a novel by Barbara Macpherson Reyelts

Looking for Lawson, a novel by Mark Kirby

About the Author

Mary Longley is a writer, having spent a great deal of her career in the legal industry. She has written about influential women and her novels focus on real life issues. *Butterflies*, a young adult novel, is her debut literary work.

Other works:

<u>Upcoming:</u>

Cult's Prey

<u>In Production - Adult:</u>

Prey's Deception

Book of Poetry

<u>In Production - Young Adult:</u>

Butterflies 2: Flying